30 years ago *The Blue Balloon* marked the moment that I began to feel like a proper children's author. It was also the first time that Kipper appeared in public, although he had not yet learned to stand on two feet as the hero of his own stories. The success of the book confirmed for me what we all understand intuitively; that playfulness is important. Even in an age of continual assessment, imagined balloons need not be constrained by the page.

Mick Inkpen

First published in Great Britain in 1989 by Hodder Children's Books
This edition published in 2019

1 3 5 7 9 10 8 6 4 2

A CIP catalogue record for this book is available from the British Library.

ISBN 978 1 44492 256 1

Printed and bound in China

Hodder Children's Books
An imprint of Hachette Children's Group
Part of Hodder and Stoughton
Carmelite House
50 Victoria Embankment
London, EC4Y 0DZ

An Hachette UK Company
www.hachette.co.uk

www.hachettechildrens.co.uk

The Blue Balloon

Mick Inkpen

The day after my birthday party Kipper found a soggy blue balloon in the garden.

It was odd because the balloons at my party were red and white.

I blew it up.

At first I thought it was
just an ordinary balloon.
But now I am not so sure.

It is shiny and squeaky and you can make rude noises with it.

And if you give it a rub you can stick it on the ceiling.

Just like an ordinary balloon.

But there is something odd about my balloon.

It doesn't matter how much you blow it up, it just goes on getting bigger . . .

and bigger until . . .

You see it never ever bursts. Never ever.

I have squeezed it . . . squashed it . . .

. . . and whacked it with a stick.

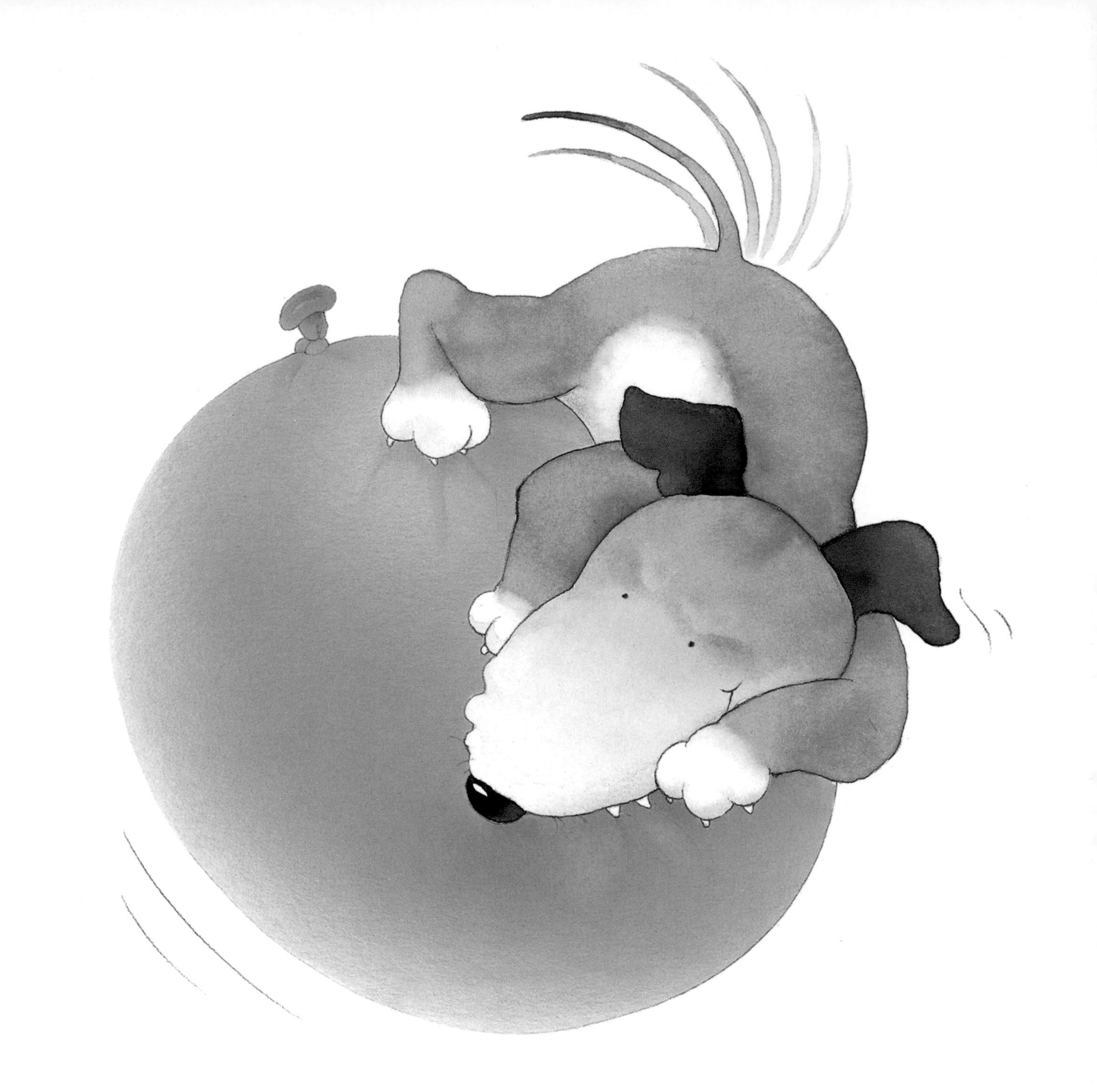

And Kipper has attacked it.
But it is Indestructible.

I have kicked it . . .   run it over . . .

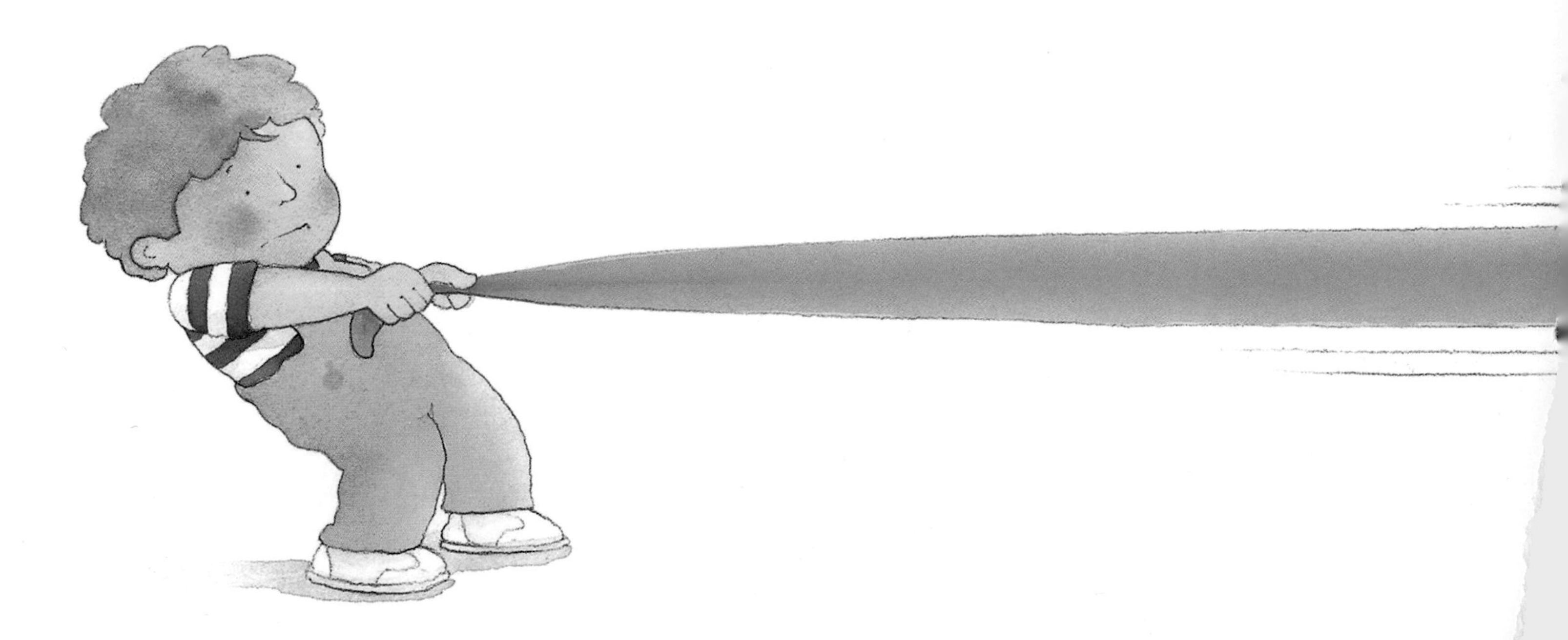

. . . and stre-e-e-e-e-e-e-e-e-e-e-e-

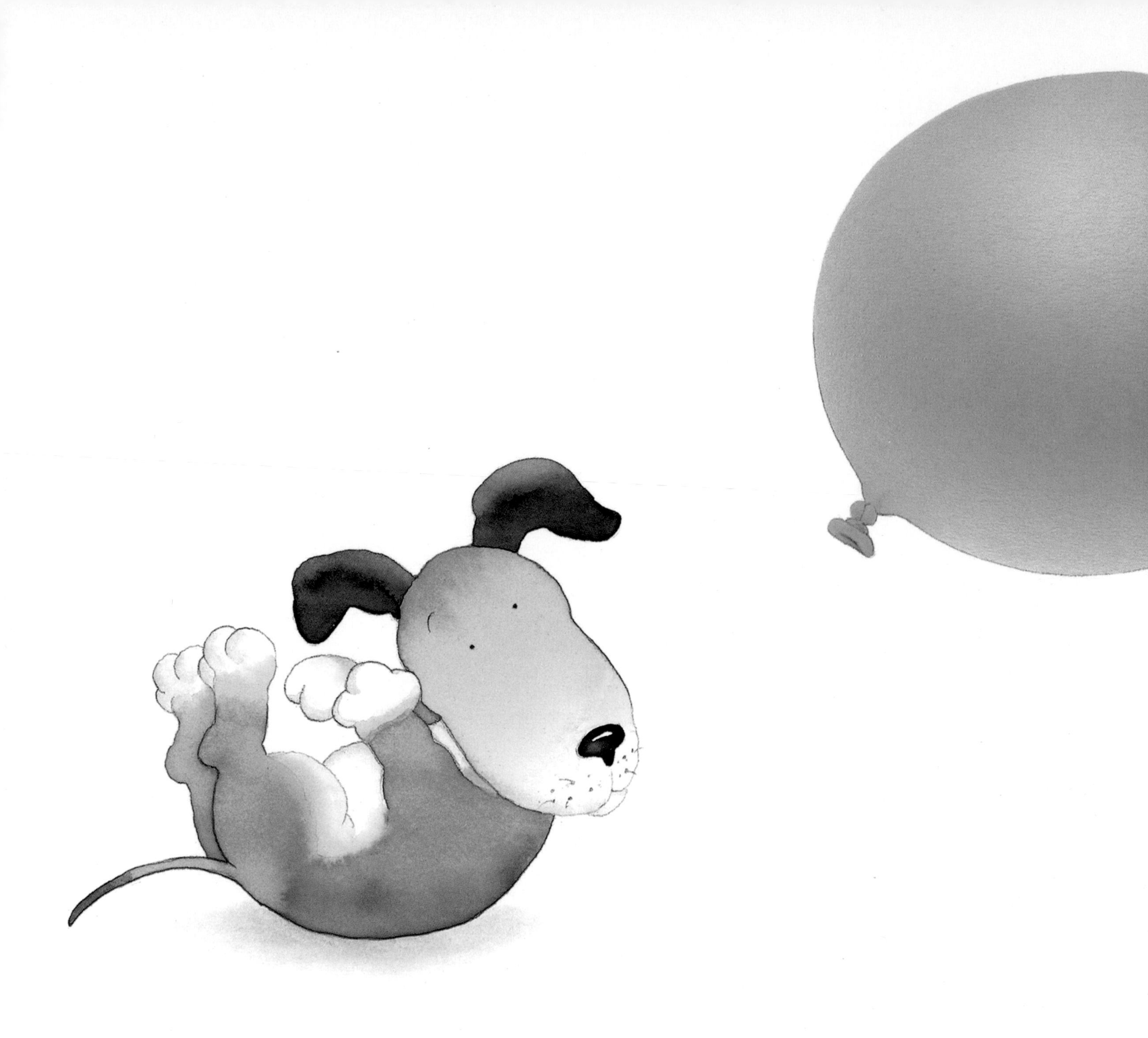

I think that my balloon has
Strange and Wonderful Powers!

The other day it disappeared completely . . .

. . . and when it came back it was square!

And this morning, while I was taking it for a walk . . .

. . . it decided to take me for a fly!

It took me up . . .

and up . . .

and up . . .

Oops!

. . . whatever you do
don't throw it away.

Especially if it's a blue one.

You never know what it will do next.

Great Kipper books to share together

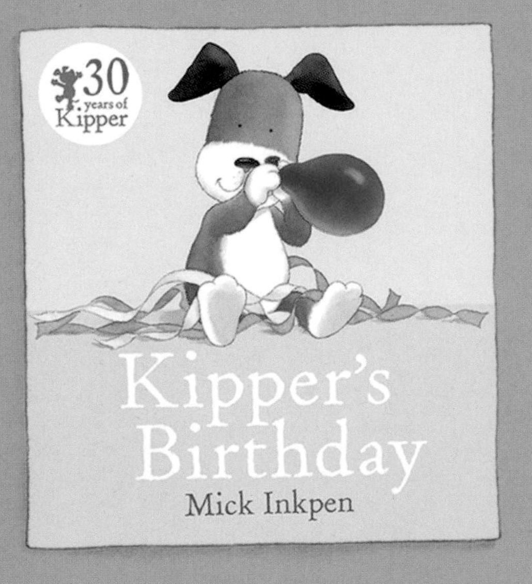

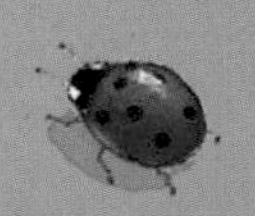

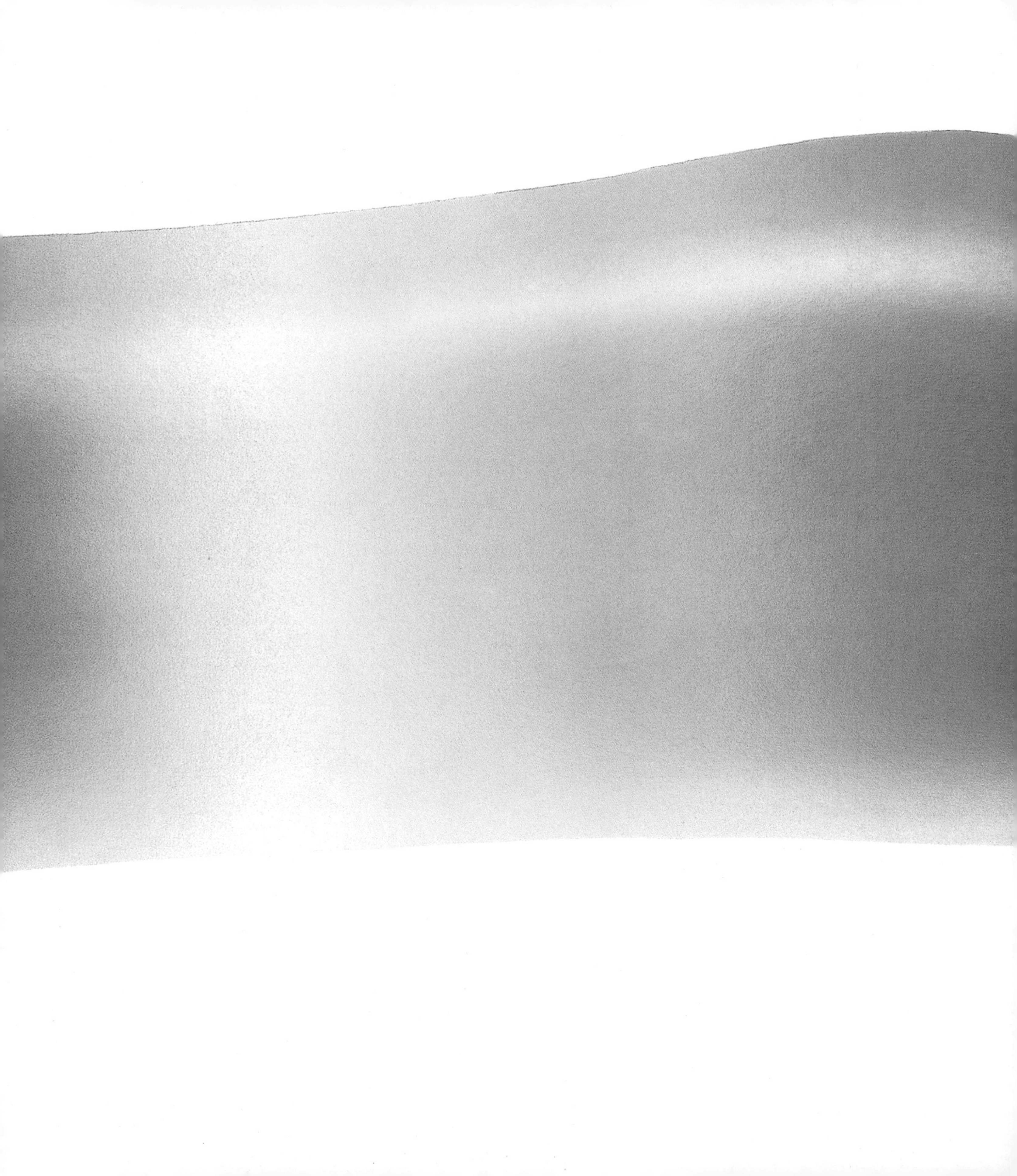

Contents

Schedules to the Regulations

Appendices to the guidance

Notices of Approval

By virtue of Section 16(1) of the Health and Safety at Work etc Act 1974 ("the 1974 Act") and with the consent of the Secretary of State for Employment, the Health and Safety Commission has on 7 December 1992 approved a Code of Practice which provides practical guidance with respect to the provisions of the Workplace (Health, Safety and Welfare) Regulations. The Code of Practice consists of those paragraphs which are identified as such in the document entitled *Workplace health, safety and welfare.*

The Code of Practice comes into effect on 1 January 1993.

Signed

T A GATES
Secretary to the Health and Safety Commission

8 December 1992

By virtue of Section 16(4) of the 1974 Act and with the consent of the Secretary of State for the Environment, the Health and Safety Commission has on 23 August 1995 approved a revision of paragraph number 147 of the Code of Practice which provides practical guidance on the provisions of the Workplace (Health, Safety and Welfare) Regulations. The said paragraph, as so revised, is included in the Code of Practice which appears in the 1995 edition of the document entitled *Workplace health, safety and welfare* and which consists of those paragraphs identified as such in that document.

The said revision to paragraph number 147 of the Code of Practice comes into effect on 23 August 1995.

Signed

T A GATES
Secretary to the Health and Safety Commission

27 September 1995